EASY READERS

The Three Little Pigs

DEAR CAREGIVER, The *Beginning-to-Read* series is a carefully written collection of classic readers you may remember from your own childhood. Each book features text comprised of common sight words to provide your child ample practice reading the words that appear most frequently in written text. The many additional details in the pictures enhance the story and offer the opportunity for you to help your child expand oral language and develop comprehension.

Begin by reading the story to your child, followed by letting him or her read familiar words and soon your child will be able to read the story independently. At each step of the way, be sure to praise your reader's efforts to build his or her confidence as an independent reader. Discuss the pictures and encourage your child to make connections between the story and his or her own life. At the end of the story, you will find reading activities and a word list that will help your child practice and strengthen beginning reading skills.

Above all, the most important part of the reading experience is to have fun and enjoy it!

Shannon Cannon

Shannon Cannon,
Literacy Consultant

Norwood House Press • P.O. Box 316598 • Chicago, Illinois 60631
For more information about Norwood House Press please visit our website at *www.norwoodhousepress.com* or call 866-565-2900.

LIBRARY OF CONGRESS CATALOGING-IN-PUBLICATION DATA

Hillert, Margaret.
    The three little pigs / by Margaret Hillert; illustrated by Irma Wilde.
— Rev. and expanded library ed.
        p. cm. — (Beginning-to-read book)
    Summary: Simple text relates the adventures of three little pigs who leave home to seek their fortunes and how they deal with the big bad wolf.
Includes reading activities.
    ISBN-13: 978-1-59953-050-5 (library binding : alk. paper)
    ISBN-10: 1-59953-050-3 (library binding : alk. paper)
    [1. Folklore. 2. Pigs—Folklore.] I. Wilde, Irma, ill. II. Title. III.
Series: Hillert, Margaret. Beginning to read series. Fairy tales and folklore.
    PZ8.1.H539Tk 2007
    398.24'529734—dc22
    [E]   2006007894

Beginning-to-Read series (c) 2007 by Margaret Hillert.
Library edition published by permission of Pearson Education, Inc. in arrangement with Norwood House Press, Inc. All rights reserved.
This book was originally published by Follett Publishing Company in 1963.

A Beginning-to-Read Book

The Three Little Pigs

by Margaret Hillert

Illustrated by Irma Wilde

NORWOOD HOUSE PRESS

Here is a pig.

Here is a pig.

And here is a pig.

One, two, three.
Three little pigs.

Three funny little pigs.

See my house.
It is a little house.
It is yellow.

Little pig, little pig.
I want to come in.

You can not.
You can not.
You can not come in.

I can puff the house down.
Puff, puff, puff.

Here is my house.
It is a funny little house.

Little pig, little pig.
I want to come in.

17

You can not.
You can not.
You can not come in.

See me puff, puff, puff.
I can puff the house down.

Look here, look here.
My house is a big one.
It is red.

Little pig, little pig.
I want to come in.

Go away.
Go away.
You can not come in.

See me puff.
I can puff.
I can puff the house down.

See here, see here.
My house is not down.

I can go up, up, up.
I can go in.

Oh my, oh my.
It is funny.
You can not go up.

You can not come down.
And you can not come in.

The following activities support the findings of the National Reading Panel that determined the most effective components for reading instruction are: Phonemic Awareness, Phonics, Vocabulary, Fluency, and Text Comprehension.

Phonemic Awareness: The /th/ sound

Substitution: Say the following words to your child and ask him or her to substitute the first sound in the word with /**th**/:

sing = thing	bird = third	jaw = thaw
bank = thank	pick = thick	sigh = thigh
crow = throw	jump = thump	wink = think
dirty = thirty	win = thin	bread = thread

Phonics: The letters Tt and Hh

1. Demonstrate how to form the letters **T**, **t**, **H**, and **h** for your child.
2. Have your child practice writing **T**, **t**, **H**, and **h** at least three times each.
3. Ask your child to point to the words on the cover of the book that start with the letters **th**.
4. Explain to your child that when we see the letters **t** and **h** together in words, they make a different sound than either letter does on its own.
5. Write down the following words and blanks and ask your child to write the letters **th** to complete each word:

    _ _ en   wi _ _   bro_ _ er   _ _ is   _ _ ing   tee_ _
    ba_ _ tub   ma_ _   _ _ em   heal_ _ y   clo_ _   pan_ _ er
6. Read each word aloud for your child, asking your child to repeat the word.
7. Randomly point to words and ask your child to read them.
8. Ask your child to spell other words with the **th** sound in them.

Vocabulary: Adjectives—Comparatives and Superlatives

1. Explain to your child that sometimes we use different forms of describing words to compare things. In order to make the describing words (adjectives) more specific, we sometimes add -er and -est to the word.

2. Write the following words on separate pieces of paper:

small   hard   cold   strong   weak   tall   smart

3. Write the suffixes er and est on separate pieces of paper.

4. Place the suffixes, one at a time, next to each word to make a new adjective. (for example: smaller, smallest)

5. Divide a piece of paper into three columns.

6. Write each word in the left column.

7. Label the middle column –er and the right column –est.

8. Help your child complete the chart by adding –er and –est to each word and write the new adjective in the appropriate column.

9. Discuss each set of words and ask your child to give examples for each. (for example: I am tall. My older sister is taller. My dad is the tallest.)

Fluency: Reader's Theater

1. Reread the story to your child at least two more times while your child tracks the print by running a finger under the words as they are read. Ask your child to read the words he or she knows with you.

2. Decide who will be the wolf, and who will be the other characters (pigs and narrator). Reread the story with each reader reading only his or her own part(s).

3. Practice reading with expression and changing voices for the characters.

Text Comprehension: Discussion Time

1. Ask your child to retell the sequence of events in the story.

2. To check comprehension, ask your child the following questions:

- What did the pigs build their houses with?
- Which houses did the wolf blow down?
- How do you think the third pig feels on page 24?
- Can you think of other things animals use to build houses?
- What would you build a house with? Why?

WORD LIST

The Three Little Pigs uses the 34 words listed below.

This list can be used to practice reading the words that appear in the text. You may wish to write the words on index cards and use them to help your child build automatic word recognition. Regular practice with these words will enhance your child's fluency in reading connected text.

a	I	pig	yellow
and	in	puff	you
away	is		
	it	red	
big			
	little	see	
can	look		
come		the	
	me	three	
down	my	to	
		two	
funny	not		
		up	
go	oh		
	one	want	
here			
house			

ABOUT THE AUTHOR Margaret Hillert has written over 80 books for children who are just learning to read. Her books have been translated into many different languages and over a million children throughout the world have read her books. She first started writing poetry as a child and has continued to write for children and adults throughout her life. A first grade teacher for 34 years, Margaret is now retired from teaching and lives in Michigan where she likes to write, take walks in the morning, and care for her three cats.

Photograph by Glenna Washburn

ABOUT THE ADVISER Shannon Cannon contributed the activities pages that appear in this book. Shannon serves as a literacy consultant and provides staff development to help improve reading instruction. She is a frequent presenter at educational conferences and workshops. Prior to this she worked as an elementary school teacher and as president of a curriculum publishing company.